Broken Signals

Jeff Friedman

BAMBOO
DART
PRESS

LOS ANGELES † NEW YORK † LONDON † MELBOURNE

Broken Signals by Jeff Friedman

978-1-947240-99-5   Paperback

978-1-947240-00-1   eBook

Cover art by Dennis Callaci

Layout and design by Mark Givens

For information:

Bamboo Dart Press

chapbooks@bamboodartpress.com

Bamboo Dart Press 048

www.pelekinesis.com   www.bamboodartpress.com   www.shrimperrecords.com

For my mother and father, Bobbie and Paul
and for my two sisters, Karen and Vicki

Contents

III

Flung into a field a long time ago, a Flute lay soundless, until one day a passing donkey blew into it, bringing forth the sweetest sound of its life—that is to say, of the Donkey's life and the Flute's life too.

—Augusto Monterrosso

Acknowledgments

My thanks to the editors of the following publications in which these poems first appeared:

Café Irreal: "House of Smoke"
Cleaver Magazine: "Card Trick"
DMQ Review: "Remembèring My Father's Face"
Emerge Literary Magazine: "Newman's Own"
50-Word Story: "Another Orpheus"
Flash Boulevard: "My Sister's Gift" and "Dog on the Roof"
The Fort Nightly Review: "Mime Love" and "My Mother's Dress Shop"
Gone Lawn: "My Father the Leopard"
Gooseberry Review: "Another Shadow"
Hole in the Head Review: "Baby Theft"
The Mackinaw: "Jitter"
Mudlark: "Chair" and "The Gift"
Northwest Review: "Almost Love"
Plume: "Sleeping Mother"
Posit: "Homeland"
South Florida Poetry Journal: "White Owl"
Spoon River Review: "Dad's Side of the Family"
Survision: The Boy at the Lake Beneath the Mountain" and "Catching the Monster"
Switch Online: "Chopsticks"

"Another Orpheus" also appeared in *The Mackinaw.* "My Mother's Dress Shop" and "Chopsticks" were selected for *Best Microfiction 2023* and *2024.* "Catching the Monster" appeared in *Prose Poem: An Introduction* published by Princeton University. "Chair" and "The Gift" were published in *Floating Tales* (Plume Editions/Madhat Press, 2017).

Thanks to Meg Pokrass, Nin Andrews, Celia Bland and Kathleen McGookey for reading this book in its various stages, for helping me to select the pieces to keep and cut, and for their insights and praise. My love and gratitude to Colleen Randall, who has lovingly lived with me and all my obsessive questions and the twists and turns of my poems, prose poems, micros and mini tales. And thanks also to editor Mark Givens for his patience, support and encouragement.

I

Remembering My Father's Face

Lying on the couch, my father disappeared like smoke through an open window. Not even his impression on the pillow remained. He had died forty years ago. I tried to remember what he looked like, but whenever I thought of him, I could only remember his tight black curly hair, his rounded shoulders, his pained feet, not his face. I tried over and over again to picture him. I saw him carrying his suitcases up the staircase, his gray fedora tilted forward, so I couldn't see his face. I saw him start his electric shaver, in his white under-shirt, but when he lifted it to shave, there was no face in the mirror, only a bright burning light. I heard him singing, "It's a quarter to three, there's nobody here...," his face a blur of chalk, an erasure, a wind lifting leaves and straw. When the leaves fell, there was only dust and air.

My Mother's Dress Shop

Break down the boxes that held the clothing and stuff them into the dumpster in the alley behind the shop. Break down the racks that held the sexy dresses, the leather coats, the French lingerie until they are just rods and wheels lying in a corner. Fold up the clothing neatly. Break down the counter, the shelves, and the cash register empty of cash. Break down the shadows that no longer hold voices. Break down the light that drops through the window like a message until it is just a scrap of light. Break down the dust that clings to the walls and counters that your mother attacks with a cloth and Windex. Break down the mannikins until they are disconnected limbs, head, and torso. Now there is only the memory of a memory, the striped cat leaping on the counter, its tail ticking back and forth, the nurses in white uniforms peeking in the windows of air to spot a skirt or blouse on sale, your mother's voice coming back to you like the smells of a fresh cinnamon sweet roll and steaming black coffee, and the blaze of sun that makes it impossible to see.

The Gift

The boy kneeled, ripping the box open, but inside the box was another box and inside that box, a smaller box, and then a smaller box. Until he came to the last box and opened it slowly. A breath of stale air rose into a small wind, circling the room until it was too big to contain and whooshed out the window. A palm full of emptiness glittered like bits of aluminum pasted on cardboard. A hush like laughter spread through the room. There was an invisible star without light, dust from old shoes with worn heels and soles, the memory of a snowflake imprinted on a window, the smell of the flood in the basement, his father and uncle sloshing through gray water in high rubber boots. There was a forgotten wish, a shredded wing, and his mother's words, "Try a little harder," and beneath it all the crumbs of a broken sugar cookie no longer sweet on the tongue.

Dad's Side of the Family

My grandmother was a fish. We kept her in a small pit filled with water in the back yard, but she never complained. My father promised her that when he hit it big, she would have a whole pool to swim around in, and her choice of the best minnows in the Midwest and a tasty selection of grains. When my grandmother came up for air, she blessed us. "I'm just happy to have my children and grandchildren," she said. But really my sister and I thought she smelled fishy, and when we hugged and kissed her, we smelled fishy also. We didn't like visiting her, but mom and dad made us go out to the pit twice a day with little gifts, sardines, pieces of chocolate, Pepperidge Farm Goldfish. We didn't really understand how our grandmother could be a fish and not a human and how she had given birth to our father. "He does have funny feet," I said to my sister, "and he loves to swim." "He looks nothing like a fish, and he doesn't smell like one either," she answered. "Maybe he was adopted," I said.

Sleeping Mother

One night at dinner, mother passed out at the table while holding her fork. The fork dropped to the floor with some greens on it. We got up, but father held out his hand to stop us. "Let her sleep," he said. Though she snored and took great gulps of breath, eventually slipping from her chair, we continued to eat our dinner. When father finished his meal, we helped him get her to bed. "I'll take care of the rest," he said. We cleaned up the kitchen and went back to our room. The next day, father hushed us. "She's still sleeping," he said. For weeks the house was silent. During the day, my father drove to work, and we took the bus to school. At night, we gathered in the bedroom, each of us kissing her. "Call the doctor," we said. "She wouldn't want that," father answered. "When it's time, she'll wake up." She looked so sweet beneath the covers, smiling after each kiss, her anger gone—her face bright and smooth as if she had shed years in her sleep.

My Sister's Gift

We're in the living room when my sister coughs up another fish. "Get that fish," my mother orders, "and throw it in the ice box." The fish flips and flops and slips out of my grasp, but eventually I trap it with a small metal wastebasket. I dump the fish in the freezer with the other fish my sister has coughed up. In the living room, my mother is reading the same book she is always reading, and my sister lies on the couch, perhaps fatigued from letting out another fish. "What's the matter with her?" I ask. "Nothing," my mother answers. "She just occasionally coughs up a fish." My sister pops up with a pillow in her hand. "Mother says I'm gifted." She giggles, proud of herself. "Don't you think we should do something about this," I ask my mother. She inserts her bookmark and places the book on the stand and then removes her black cat-eye glasses. "Why," she says, "the fish are pretty good, dinner-sized and tasty. Your sister is saving us money on our grocery bill with her gift." "What if she coughs up a fish at school," I ask. "Everyone will ridicule her mercilessly." My sister punches me on the arm softly. "No, they won't. You should see some of the things they cough up." My mother tells me to mind my own business and that it wouldn't hurt me to contribute something to the family budget. Then I feel a tickling in my throat and a cough trying to leap out, so I keep my mouth shut for the rest of the morning.

My Father the Leopard

My Father was a leopard. He was gone all night and slinked in just before dawn. I imagined him lying on a long tree branch, his yellow eyes drinking in the moon, his spotted tail barely visible as he waited for his prey to come to him. He would sleep all day, and I would walk quietly up to him, breathe his fierce breath and dreams. "Leave him be," my mother would say. "He needs his rest." If I touched his arm or shoulder, he'd wake just long enough to swat me across the room with his powerful paw. "He loves you in his way," my mother told me, "but don't test him." Even sleeping, his majestic face was still frightening, and the whole house wasn't big enough for his angry growl.

Floozy

After our father died, our mother told us that, he used to drive around in a little red roadster with a floozy from Memphis, that they skinny-dipped in a pond and drank whiskey like crazy. She revealed that they had gotten married and had two kids. "Why didn't you tell us this before?" She clicked her tongue. "Your father was a secretive man. He didn't think you needed to know. "I want to meet them," my sister said. My mother shook her head. "Not necessary. I was the floozy."

Smaller and Smaller Pieces

In his bedroom room, long after midnight, the boy holds a small flashlight over his comic book, trying to read himself to sleep. He hears his father snoring in front of the TV in the living room. He hears his mother's Book of the Month Club selection fall on the floor as she dozes off.

*

In his parents' bedroom, the boy finds three quarters on his mother's dresser—heads, tails, heads. He closes one eye, stands each one on edge and flicks them with his middle finger, until all three spin at once.

*

Now, his father gone on a long sales trip, the boy finds a crumpled piece of paper with a smear of ink where he has written a secret message, but then blotted it out after committing it to memory, like a spy on an urgent mission. He recites the message and rips the paper into smaller and smaller pieces, throwing them into the air—graffiti showering over him.

*

In the kitchen, he finds the bright sun, his mother's plant on the sill, a blue window—so much empty space he wonders how he can ever fill it.

Our Son Moves Back In

He wanted a 52-inch screen, a sound system, a trumpet and drum set, so we gave it to him. He hugged us both, and we felt good. In a short while, he began blowing awful screeches through the trumpet and beating on the drums night and day. He wouldn't leave his room, and if we knocked, "He'd shout, "Don't come in." Then he wanted his own wing of the house, so we gave him the upper level. Then he began to smash beer cans and bottles, break chairs against the walls. We climbed the stairs slowly. "What's the matter," we asked. "You're the matter," he answered. "Quit asking me that." Then he wanted the whole house, so we moved into the shed out back. At night he cranked up the sound system and banged on his drums. The noise spilled out into the yard like water overflowing a sink. The house vibrated until the windows cracked. The neighbors complained. The police came, but then the house went silent and dark. When they left, we knocked on the door and rang the doorbell persistently. He opened the window and shouted down, "I'm not happy!" Then he lit a flame in an empty milk bottle.

Fly Chaser

The baby is crying again, but a fat blue fly buzzes around her head and she reaches her hand out as if trying to catch it. The fly lands on her belly. The baby laughs as the fly tickles her with its many legs. "Do something," my wife says, lounging on the couch, so I pick up the swatter and go after the fly. While I lean over the crib, the baby giggles and gurgles, the fly crawling on her belly. For a moment, the fly bunches up, at rest, the baby cooing. For a moment, there is peace. "Do something," my wife repeats, and the fly, sensing a threat, springs up, grazing my cheek. I chase after it, swatting the air numerous times until my wife grabs the swatter from me; the fly, sensing a more formidable foe, rises to the ceiling, clinging to the tiles with its sticky feet, upside down. My wife leaps up several times swinging, but misses. Now the baby is crying again, even louder than before, and we both rush to her rescue, the fly swooping in behind us.

Shrinking Son

Our son is shrinking. A week ago, he was outgrowing his clothing, but then his clothing swallowed him. He crawled out of his jeans and up the leg of the couch. A few days ago, I could get both hands around his waist; now I can hold him in the palm of my hand. "Do something," my wife shouts, so I pick him up again and hold him. He seems no smaller than he was a few hours ago. "He's holding steady," I say. "We may be turning a corner." She pulls out the tape measure. "Not again," I say, but she measures him from head to toe and around the waist. "He's lost an eighth of an inch," she says. "That could just be where you placed your thumb," I say. "He looks the same to me." "He always looks the same to you," she answers. She calls the doctor again. "Give him more to eat," the doctor says, "more beef. He's a teenager. He needs the protein to grow." We cook a steak and potatoes. Our son stands on the plate barely as tall as the roasted potato. We cut it up and watch him nibble the food. He seems in good spirits. "That's all I can eat," he says. "Let's weigh him again," she says, so we weigh him, 6 ounces. "He's lost two ounces," she says and runs to the medicine cabinet to get his anti-shrinking medicine. She pours drops of the red liquid in a saucer. He kneels down to lick it up. "That should do for now," I say, but later while I hold him in my palm, he disappears, so small he's only a tiny voice, only so many atoms clinging to each other. And then the voice is gone. "Don't close your hands," my wife commands, "and never wash them."

Baby Theft

The mother and father were fighting again, arguing over who was at fault for all their problems. They had stepped away from the baby carriage to yell at each other when a hawk swooped down, lifted the baby out of the stroller, and flew away. At first, the mother and father didn't notice, but when they finally stopped arguing, they saw that the baby was missing, which caused them to start arguing again, shouting blame at each other. The hawk carried the baby into the branches of the oak and laid it in a large twiggy nest. When the baby awoke and saw the hawk, it let out a series of high-pitched calls and shrieks until the hawk tickled its body with its beak, and then the baby laughed, its wings just beginning to open.

The Boy at the Lake Beneath the Mountain

The boy threw a stone into the water and barely cracked the surface. Certainly he could do better than that. He picked up a rock and pitched it harder, and the water rose a few feet before the rock disappeared. Then he picked up a larger rock and hurled it. A fountain of water rose forty feet and fell soaking him. Now he was pleased with himself and confident. Next, he found a huge boulder, picked it up and carried it to the edge of the shore. Hoisting it over his head with a sudden strength, he heaved it into the belly of the water, and this time the whole lake flew into the sky, hovering over the boy as he ran through the crater gathering shells and coins as quickly as he could.

II

House of Smoke

My lover and I lived in a house of smoke. At first it was just a few wisps, but with time, the smoke grew so thick I couldn't see her. Sometimes, I thought she was close to me, but when I reached out to touch her, my hand touched an empty bed or the couch cushion. Sometimes, I would call out to her to come to me. My voice fell at my feet, muted. I thought I could hear her in the distance, but her words were too faint to make out. I parted the smoke with my hands over and over, but it always filled in thicker. Sometimes I thought I saw a shadow in the smoke like a woman trapped inside a bubble. When the winds came and blew our house away, all that remained was ash sparkling in the sun and the echo of a lovely voice—gone for so many years.

Almost Love

White Wings

She thought she had white wings. I didn't see any wings anywhere, but I didn't want to disagree. "They're beautiful wings," I said, "but really they have a bit of yellow and blue in them." "Yes, I like that," she said and lifted both of her arms as if ready to embrace me or fly away.

Purple Ribbons

I gave her a purple ribbon that I found at a table in the bar. She took the ribbon and stared at it for a moment. "Thank you," she said. "You must think I'm an angel." Then she walked across the room and dropped it in the garbage can.

Salty

She said my lips were salty. I said her lips were salty, which is why she thought my lips were salty. She shook her head. "You're the saltiest person I know; it's as if you were dipped in seawater."

Loop

She looped the ribbon around a swath of her hair and tied it. I touched her cheek, ready to kiss her, but then my hand reached up to pull the ribbon loose. She grabbed my hand. "Uh uh," she said. "That's there for a reason. Not sure about you." She let go of my hand. "Are we back to this again?" I asked. "Back to what," she said. "The same old loop," I answered. She removed the ribbon and tossed it toward me; it floated between us like an unanswered kiss.

Sleepwalking

My lover sleepwalks after midnight, leaving a trail of open doors behind her. If I clasp her arm to bring her back, she stops momentarily to lift my hand off and continues on as if I had never touched her. She has yet to fall down steps or stumble on the sidewalk. She parts the night as if wading through shallow water. When a car comes, she waits on the corner. Sometimes I walk beside her to see the brightness of her face as if the moon is lighting it. "Where are we going," I ask. "I'll know when we get there," she answers, but she's not awake. And sometimes I follow her to see if she will wait for me, but she just keeps going, no matter how far I fall behind. At such times, I hurry to catch up, fearing that a tree might reach for her with its long limbs or a dark bird might snatch her with its beak or the chunks of a dying star might crash down on her, but nothing like that happens. Instead, she stops and gathers the wind in her mouth, blowing into the darkness until it is even darker. Then she follows the shadows through the open doors, and I close them behind her.

Mime Love

When I was young, I fell in love with a mime, who loved me back, but never actually touched me. She would deliver her love from a distance, moving her body sinuously as if she had no bones. Sometimes she would draw pictures of her love for me on a window that didn't exist. She kissed the air and pointed at me. She tapped her heart with her hand and seemed to melt. She would reach out and mime tugging a rope to pull me toward her. But if I would actually walk toward her, she backed into a shadow and remained so still I wasn't even sure she was in the room. "Why don't we ever make love?" I asked. "We do make love," she answered, speaking with her hands. Once, I watched her pantomime our lovemaking, playing both parts, herself and me. She was so good I could feel a shiver run through my body, so good I was almost happy.

Gift

My lover gave me a box wrapped in pretty red ribbon. When I ripped it open, there was another box and inside that box a tray shiny with chocolates, an assortment of chocolates. "You get back what you give," she said. I had bought these same chocolates for her. She was regifting my gift. "But shouldn't we get what we want?" I asked. "Then you should buy your own gift," she answered. She picked out a chocolate and placed it in my hand. "Nice," I said smelling it before biting in. The chocolate shell cracked, and the ganache tasted so sweet I felt a little dizzy, but I wanted another. "I knew you would like this gift," she said. I ate another chocolate and then another, and now I was no longer dizzy, just eager for more. "Slow up," she said. "You'll get sick." "Have one," I said. She tasted hers, letting it sit on her tongue and closing her eyes while I finished three more. "They're delicious," she said, "but I don't really like dark chocolate." "Have another," I said; "No, they're yours," she said. "I didn't get them for me." She plucked the empty wrappers out of the box and tossed them in the garbage can. "I'll buy you a gift," I said. "What would you like?" "You figure it out," she answered, "Surprise me." Maybe some chocolates, I thought and kept eating until I finished every last one. Then my belly filled with a great emptiness, and there was nothing left to eat.

Chair

When the man rises from a chair, after reading the newspaper, his body is shaped like a chair. Must be stiffness from sitting so long, he thinks, and stretches toward the ceiling, but his arms won't reach and his lower half squats. He shouts for his wife to help him. She sweeps in from the kitchen. "What's wrong," she asks. "I'm shaped like a chair," he says. "You've been hunching down like that for a while now," she answers and sits on his lap. "And you're very comfortable." "I can't go to work like this," he says. "Why not?" she asks. "You sit all day. No one will notice, and besides you're off for the week, so don't worry." She brushes her lips against his. She kisses his nubby cheek, purring. "Your upholstery is lovely," she says. "It's not funny," he snaps and tries to get up, but his wife yawns and stretches her legs over his arms, settling in for a nice long nap.

Voice

Her voice spoke softly and kindly, floating up from her diaphragm past her teeth and lips, drifting among the dust particles like a beam of light. If I closed my eyes, I could smell her voice, warm like cinnamon. And even when she wasn't speaking, I could hear her, even when I was asleep and the night birds entered my dreams. And one day, I slipped down inside her and swallowed her voice. Now she was silent, though her lips moved, though her hands gesticulated as if she were singing. The two voices lived inside me, like wings stirring up the wind, brushing the bars of their cage. And I would speak to her sometimes in my voice and sometimes in hers. In truth, I could no longer tell the difference. I was never sure what she heard, but sometimes she wept as if the stars were speaking to her. Then she would kiss me on the lips as if slipping me a message with her tongue.

Chopsticks

How he loved remembering that she had been in love with him, kissing him suddenly while they sat at the piano, playing Chopsticks together. She didn't remember that: kissing him or being in love. *I would never have played Chopsticks, or any other song with you. I never learned to play the piano,* she said. He took her hands in his and looked into her eyes. *We were lovers,* he said. *I just met you,* she answered. He led her to the piano and helped her sit down. *We've been married a long time,* he said, taking the spot next to her. She closed her eyes, thinking about what he had just told her, but when she thought about lying down in the bedroom, she couldn't picture him beside her. When she thought about the living room, he was not in it. Nor was he with her when she walked the neighborhood, stopping to admire the purple flowers and the Burning Bushes. Nor could she place him in the garden. Nor could she feel his lips kissing her tenderly on the cheek. As he began to play "Chopsticks," her hands moved up and down too, but didn't touch the keys.

Broken Signals

My wife's hand shakes when she tries to twist off a jar lid or when she holds the kettle and pours the hot water to make tea. Her hand shakes when she applies her muted lipstick in front of the mirror, leaving a slight smear above her upper lip. It shakes when she brushes her long blond hair with a nylon brush passing it through numbers of times; then she tugs out the hairs from the brush bristles and twines them around her fingers. And when she touches my cheek, her hand shakes. Sometimes I press it into mine, and the quivering enters my body. I can feel it rushing all the way to my feet, down into the floor. I tremble for her. Then her hand remains still like an ear waiting to catch the next wave of broken signals.

Jitter

Even when we weren't on speed, Rachel and I were always jittery as though lights flickered inside us. When we weren't doing speed, we drank coffee black, not fancy coffee either, Maxwell House or the kind you get in a coffee shop early in the morning. Our friend Jimmy dealt cocaine, and he paid us to make deliveries to his clientele. Our hands shook exchanging the packets of powder for cash. Jimmy sold us the speed at a discount. Rachel would poke the syringe into my vein and then hit up herself. Even our bodies, even the night, couldn't contain us. We shared everything, a bed, Cheerios, cheese sandwiches, cash, credit cards, sweatshirts, needles, even hepatitis.

Card Trick

Though it was warm in the house, Callie covered herself to the neck with an afghan and lay down on the couch. Her red and green wool socks pushed out into the open. "Can I bring you something," I asked. She shook her head. "How about a glass of wine? Maybe that will make you feel better." She didn't say "No," so I poured a glass of merlot and placed it on the coffee table. Then I got my deck of cards. "Pick a card," I said, holding the deck near her hands. She picked her card and held it up to her face and then when I opened the deck, she slipped it in. "Are you ready," I asked. She looked tired and weak. "Va voo, va voo," I said and fanned the deck again as I opened my hands. The deck floated above us, all 52 cards spread out, but still touching each other. I plucked the card from the deck as it floated. "Queen of Diamonds," I said. A hint of a smile on her lips, "It's not my card," she said and closed her eyes.

III

After the Surgery

There's a hole in my head from the surgery, not a large hole, but large enough for a tall person to peek down into it and see the soup simmering in pots on the stovetop. The vapors rise from the hole, spreading around me until trees, houses and cars look a little blurry. I zig zag around the block numerous times trying to navigate a straighter path. Soon, I'm in a thick fog of my own, and the neighbors walking their dogs or jogging with headphones embedded in their ears like batteries don't see me. Memories float out of the hole in my head like filaments of hair or dust particles catching the light. What were they? I wish I knew. So much is being lost that when I get home, I stuff the hole with cotton pads and tape over it. But the soup begins to boil; the tape comes loose; and the memories pitch themselves up, evaporating in the bright air.

My Inner Voice

My inner voice complains that I always cut him off, but if I don't, he just keeps talking. And when I interrupt, he shouts, "Let me finish." Of course, when I'm talking, he feels free to break in and take over. His voice is high, shrill, always scolding, "You really screwed that up. You call that a job well done? Go back and clean up your mess." Wise men say that you should listen to your inner voice, but they probably have wise inner voices. Mine seems ill informed and a little fanatical. It is possible that my inner voice was intended for a different body, for someone else. But then why has no one come to claim him? Often, angry with me for ignoring what he has to say or not following his advice, he lapses into silence. I coax him to speak by making promises: "I won't interrupt. Talk as long as you want. I'll do what you tell me to do." I feel him inside me, nodding his head. He laughs loudly.

Newman's Own

My lover thought I was Paul Newman, which is probably why she became my lover. One night in bed, I told her the truth. "I'm not Paul Newman." She started to laugh. "You're a joker all right," she said. "No, really! Paul Newman has blue eyes that are clear as skies. I've got dark beady brown eyes, Hungarian eyes. He has a square jaw, and I have a weak chin partially hidden by a scraggly beard. I've never made love to Liz Taylor or Dominique Sanda or Joanne Woodward, and I don't drink two six packs in two months, let alone two hours." "Well, she said, "your tomato sauce is pretty good."

Spanish Fly

At thirteen, Benny Kodner and I were in a cab on the way to see The Supremes in concert. The cab driver, an obese man in a Hawaiian print shirt, kept making small talk, then for no apparent reason pulled to the curb and turned around. "Do you want your girl to go crazy for you?" he asked. We both had girlfriends, but neither of us could say they were crazy for us. In fact, I had only occasionally made out with my girlfriend, mostly just held hands. He held up a vial of green fluid and shook it a little. It splashed against the glass. "A few drops of this in her drink, and she'll do anything you want," he said, "putty in your hands." I wasn't sure what that might mean. "I can give you a vial for 25 bucks each. The best 25 bucks you'll ever spend." He kept his eyes on us in the rear-view mirror. "I only have two of these left, so if you want them, speak up now." He scratched his neck until it turned red. He had a stubbly wide face. Benny looked away, but I said "No," softly—afraid that we might look weak to him. "Mister, we don't have the cash." He shook his head, "You guys'll never get laid," he said and pulled away from the curb.

Another Shadow

Hunger is eating my daughter. Driving from state to state, she lives on trail mix and Kind Bars—frail as the memory of a father long gone. She hears my voice whispering to her, telling her to stop, to eat a meal and fill her emptiness, telling her to love someone and let herself be loved. She doesn't know who is speaking or if she is only imagining my voice. Speeding on the highway, she sticks her head out and swallows the wind as if feeding herself on air. In each town, she looks for another shadow to be her father.

The Dog on the Roof

The dog pants near the bottom of the sloping roof. He neither stands nor sits, but crouches as if he feels himself about to slide. He looks down and sees shadows in motion. Perhaps sensing the dog watching from above, a cat sneaks across the street and then disappears behind the overflowing garbage cans. The sun warms the dog's face as he smells the rotting meat and pizza crusts. He doesn't bark at the bodies moving below. His ears flick when the flies touch them. The wind brings him so many messages and signals he can hardly contain himself, his nose in constant motion, his tail whipping back and forth. The crowd gathers, watching the dog. "Stay," they shout. "We'll rescue you," but the dog slowly backs up the slope until he's almost at the chimney. "Then he springs forward, leaping off the roof, his four legs spreading apart, as everyone below tilts their heads and watches. Instead of falling, the dog rises until it disappears into a cloud. And one by one, the clouds float toward the horizon, each with a tail ticking behind it.

The Boy on the Roof

The boy stood on the roof, watching the crowd gather beneath him. Up here, he was happy. He could see a large brown dog pillaging a garbage can whose silvery top had fallen off. Pigeons were scavenging the scraps of food on the street, and a small gray cat peeked out of one alley and darted across the street to another. The boy stuck his foot out over the ledge as if testing the temperature of water in a pool or lake, then he pulled it back. "Don't jump," people shouted. He smiled at them. The sun warmed his face. There wasn't even the slightest breath of wind. Many in the crowd were talking on their cellphones. He heard a siren, and the dog almost fell into the garbage can before it ran off. A red truck and a car pulled up. Men with helmets got out. They pushed their way through and spread out a net. "Stay where you are," one shouted. "Someone's coming to help you. "These are my wings," he said holding up his arms. He saw a man entering the door to the building. The boy backed up. Running, he spread his arms and flew off the roof and sailed over the crowd while the men with the net spread it as wide as it would go and scrambled to get under him.

Another Orpheus

"Isn't this cozy?" I said. "We're in a box," she answered. "I want out." The sun shone in the window, and a rainbow fell across her face. Over the years, our house had grown small. I pulled out a matchstick and played my tiny violin. Even the dust listened.

White Owl

In my dream, a white owl flew into our house and landed on the ceiling beam. "Do something about him," my wife said. "How do you know it's male?" I asked. She squinched her face angrily "You left the window open again," she said. "I told you not to." But the window was shut, and there was no broken glass. The owl scanned the room emitting a menacing call. "Owls are supposed to be wise," I said. "Maybe it'll tell us something important." "Owls are dangerous," she said. "It's dangerous to believe them." The owl shook several times, then plunged as if it spotted a small bird or a mouse. We tracked the white owl from room to room, but it hid from us and didn't make a sound. "We'll never be able to sleep or have a moment's peace with that owl in the house," she said. "But we are asleep," I said, opening my long white wings.

Homeland

"You should visit Hungary," my sister said. "It's our homeland." "How can it be my homeland?" I asked. "I've never been there." "Everyone there has dad's brown eyes and his rock of a chin." Everyone looks like him and like us." I peered into my sister's face and saw my father's face and then my own. I remembered how my father combed Wildroot into his black curly hair, huffing so forcefully he fogged up the bathroom mirror, how he whipped the comb away, flinging oily drops on the tile floor, how at dinner he inhaled the hot breath of Hungarian stew as though it were the air rising from the earth of his homeland. A country of our people, I thought, everyone looking like everyone else, everyone looking like us— every face a mirror of every face. "Scary, I said. "I'm not going."

About the Author

JEFF FRIEDMAN is the author of ten collections of poetry and prose, including *Ashes in Paradise* (Madhat Press, November 2023), *The House of Grana Padano* (Pelekinesis, April 2022, cowritten with Meg Pokrass), *The Marksman* (Carnegie Mellon University Press, 2020), and *Floating Tales* (Plume Editions/Madhat Press, 2017). Friedman's work has appeared in *American Poetry Review, Poetry, New England Review, Cast-Iron Aeroplanes That Can Actually Fly: Commentaries from 80 American Poets on their Prose Poetry, Flash Fiction Funny, Flash Nonfiction Funny, Dreaming Awake: New Contemporary Prose Poetry from the United States, Australia and the United Kingdom, The New Republic,* and *Best*

Microfiction 2021, 2022, 2023 and *2024.* He has received an NEA Literature Translation Fellowship, two individual Artist Grants from New Hampshire Arts Council. and numerous other awards and prizes.

Friedman is married to the painter Colleen Randall, and they live with their dog Ruby, a mini Aussie, in West Lebanon, New Hampshire. He can often be seen in a large Wallaroo wide-brimmed hat and sunglasses walking 7-10 miles every day with Ruby, whose wondrous barking has become renowned all over New Hampshire and across the border in Vermont.

https://poetjefffriedman.com

112 N. Harvard Ave. #65

Claremont, CA 91711

chapbooks@bamboodartpress.com

www.bamboodartpress.com